The Lad Who Made the Princess Laugh

A FOLK TALE FROM GERMANY

retold by Jane Belk Moncure
illustrated by Lois Axeman

THE
CHILD'S
WORLD

ELGIN, ILLINOIS 60120

Original Folk Tale — "The Golden Goose"

Library of Congress Cataloging in Publication Data

Moncure, Jane Belk.
  The lad who made the princess laugh.

  SUMMARY: Retells the tale of the peasant lad whose
generosity brought him great rewards.
  1. Fairy tales.   2. Folklore—Germany   I. Axeman,
Lois.   II. Title.
PZ8.M753Lad   398.2'1'0943   E   79-25835
ISBN 0-89565-109-2

Distributed by Childrens Press, 1224 West Van Buren Street,
Chicago, Illinois 60607.

There once was a princess who would not
laugh. She would not even smile. After
awhile, she made everyone in the palace
sad. The king was sad. The queen was sad.
The ladies-in-waiting were sad. Why, even
the cook was sad.

"What shall we do?" asked the queen one day. "We must find a way to make the princess laugh. Her frowning casts a spell over me."

"I'll declare a Laughing Day," said the king. "People can come and try to make the princess laugh. Anyone who can make the princess laugh shall have half my kingdom."

That very day the king sent messengers throughout the land to spread the news.

A poor woodcutter heard the news. He gathered his sons around him.

"Now hear this," he said to the oldest son, and he told about the Laughing Day. "Chop your wood for the day," he said. "Then you may go to the palace and make the princess laugh."

"How can I do that?" asked the oldest son, yawning.

"Stand on your head," said his father. "Something! Anything! Just make her laugh!"

The oldest son took his ax and left. As he went out the door, his mother gave him a sweet cake for lunch.

No sooner had the oldest son entered the woods than he met a dwarf.

"Please give me a piece of cake," said the dwarf. "For I am hungry."

"No, indeed!" said the oldest son. "Why should I? This is my cake! Now go away!"

At that, the dwarf disappeared.

The oldest son picked a tree and began to chop at it. But it was a very tough tree. The oldest son chopped and chopped. No matter how hard he worked, the tree would not fall down.

Finally, the young man became so angry, he hit the tree with a mighty blow! But all he did was break his ax. The young man stamped his feet and went home to fix the ax.

"With that frown, you could never make the princess laugh," said the woodcutter. He then sent his second son into the woods. The mother gave her son bread and cheese to take along for lunch.

No sooner had the second son entered the woods than he, too, met the dwarf.

"Please give me some of your bread and cheese," said the dwarf. "For I am very hungry."

"Share my lunch with you? Never!" said the second son.

The dwarf disappeared, and the second son picked a tree to chop. This tree also was very tough. The second son chopped and chopped.

Finally, in anger, he hit the tree with a mighty blow. But the ax bounced off and hit his toe!

Hopping on one foot, and frowning a mighty frown, the second son returned home.

"With that frown, you could never make the princess laugh!" said the woodcutter.

"Please, Father," begged the youngest son. "Let me go. I know I can chop wood. I know I can make the princess laugh. Just let me try."

"You are too young to use the ax," said his father.

"You are too weak to carry a log," said the oldest son.

"The princess will tease you and call you a dummling," said the second son. And the two older sons laughed and laughed at their younger bother.

But the young lad begged and begged. Finally, the woodcutter threw up his hands.

"Go, if you must!" he said.

The lad's mother gave him an end crust from a left-over, dried-up loaf of bread. That was all she had left to eat.

As soon as the young lad entered the woods, he, too, met the dwarf.

"Please give me some food," said the dwarf. "For I am very hungry."

"Kind sir," said the lad, "I have only dry bread. But I will share what I have with you."

The dwarf and the lad sat under a giant tree and ate together. When they had finished, the dwarf said, "Since you shared with me, I will give you a magic blessing. Cut down this giant tree. Beneath it, you will find a treasure. Take the treasure to the princess."

And once more, the dwarf disappeared. The lad went right to work and chopped down the tree. As it fell, he saw a hole in the trunk. He reached down and pulled out a golden goose.

"Well, well," he said. "You are a treasure indeed! A treasure fit for the princess."

Away he marched, down the road, with the golden goose under his arm.

At this very moment, a circus parade was also marching along the road.

"Look at that golden goose," called a clown. "I wish it were mine." He reached over to touch the goose.

Now the golden goose had magic powers. So when the clown touched the goose, the clown could not get loose.

"Hey, wait! What's wrong here?" said the clown.

Then an elephant tried to rescue the clown by picking him up. Now the elephant could not get loose. The lad just kept walking along, singing a silly song.

At that point, a lion jumped up on the elephant, who was holding the clown, who was grabbing the goose, who was being carried by the lad. Now the lion could not get loose.

Two monkeys with umbrellas jumped upon the lion and elephant. Alas! Alack! They stuck too!

The lad with the goose kept marching along, singing a silly song. And behind him came the clown, the elephant, the lion, and the two monkeys with umbrellas.

"Hey!" said the circus owner, "where are you taking my animals?" He grabbed the elephant's tail and he, too, was stuck!

"Help me! Help me!" he shouted. The ring master, the trapeze artist, and the strong man all ran to help. And all three were stuck!

As if nothing had happened at all, the lad marched along. He still carried his golden goose. He still sang his silly song. And behind him came the clown, the elephant, the lion, and the two monkeys.

Behind the elephant came the circus owner, the ring master, the trapeze artist, and the strong man. And all of them shouted! And all of them struggled, trying to get loose!

Oh, what a sight they were! Everyone who saw them laughed and laughed and laughed.

The woodcutter's youngest son marched right up to the palace steps.

"May I see the princess please?" he asked.

Soon the princess saw the ridiculous parade. Though she tried not to, she started to smile. Then the smile broke into a laugh. She laughed and laughed and laughed. She laughed so loudly, she woke up the king from his nap.

The king was so happy! Then and there, he made the lad a prince—and gave him half of the kingdom!

"Golden goose," said the lad, "you can let
the parade go now."

So the goose did. Then the whole royal
family, including the lad-made-prince and
his golden goose, went to the circus
together, laughing as they went.

DATE DUE

MAY 10 '80	SEP 2 5 2003	
JUL 1 '80	JUL 27 2005	
JUL 19 '80	OCT 12 2007	
JAN 10 '81		
AUG 18 '81		
JUN 8 '82		
MAR 19 '83		
APR 19 '83		
OCT 9 '84		
FEB 2 2 1985		
APR 6 1985		
AUG 2 0 1985		
NOV 2 1985		
JUL 2 2 1986		
DEC 1 3 1988		
MAR 3 1998		
JUL 2 3 1998		
MAR 0 4 1999		
GAYLORD		PRINTED IN U.S.A.